For John

My special thanks to the staff at Illumination Arts for putting their hearts into every book they publish. And thank you to my friends and family for their enthusiastic and unconditional support.

Wendy Stofan Halley

These illustrations are dedicated to the "shiny spirit" within every human being upon our beautiful planet.

Roberta Collier-Morales

INSIDE OUT

Story by Wendy Stofan Halley

Illustrations by Roberta Collier-Morales

ILLUMINATION Arts

PUBLISHING COMPANY, INC.
BELLEVUE, WASHINGTON

Karly had a magical life. Every day she laughed and played with her special friend, Natasha. They pretended to jump on clouds and walk on the moon. They bounced on the bed like kangaroos. And sometimes they even rolled around like leaves blowing in the wind.

Playing with Natasha was Karly's favorite thing to do.

One day, Karly and Natasha had a tea party. There
were chocolate swirl cookies, blueberry pie and vanilla ice cream
sandwiches. Karly's mother came out and poured a cup of sweet
cinnamon tea with milk.

"Mom, you forgot to give Natasha some tea."

"Oh, I'm sorry, Pumpkin. I didn't see her," Mom said.
She poured another cup of tea and went back inside.

"Why can't my mom see you?" Karly asked.

"Only you can see me," Natasha said. "I'm your invisible friend."

"What do you mean?"

Natasha dunked a chocolate swirl cookie into her tea. "I don't have a body like you do. I'm a spirit, silly!"

Karly's eyes got big. "A spirit? You mean a ghost?"

"Oh no!" Natasha said. "I'm not a ghost. A spirit is kind of like an angel without wings." She sighed. "I like wings. I wish I had wings."

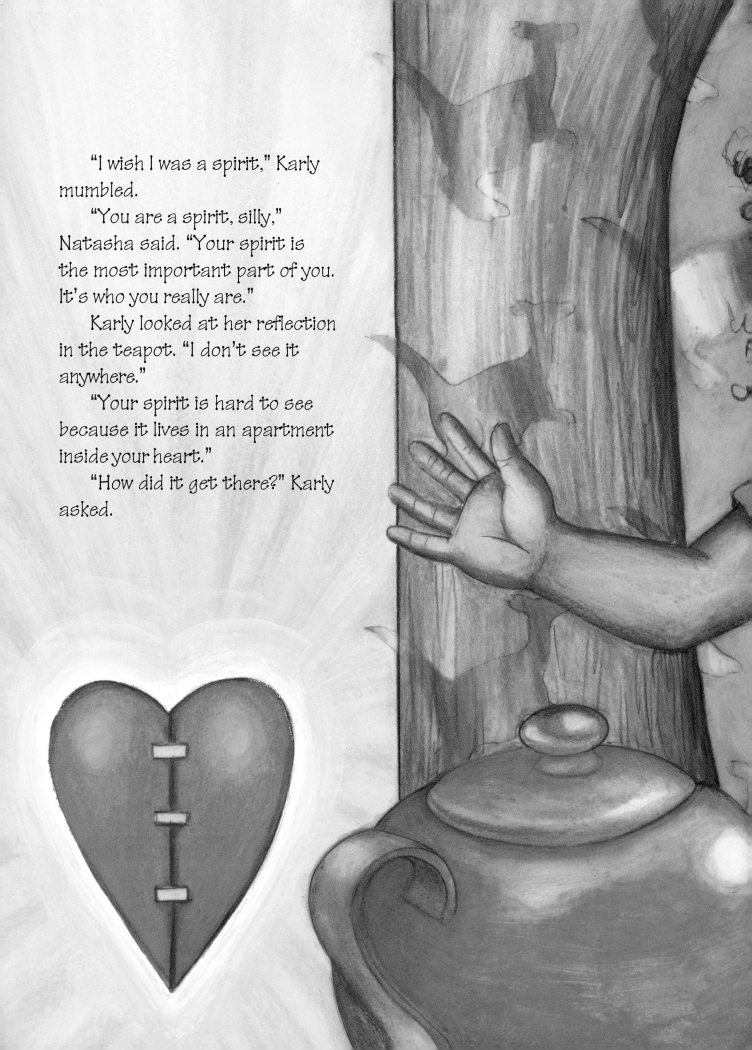

"I wish I was a spirit," Karly mumbled.

"You are a spirit, silly," Natasha said. "Your spirit is the most important part of you. It's who you really are."

Karly looked at her reflection in the teapot. "I don't see it anywhere."

"Your spirit is hard to see because it lives in an apartment inside your heart."

"How did it get there?" Karly asked.

Natasha took Karly by the hand
and they sat under a shady tree.
   "Let me tell you a story," Natasha said.
   "Once upon a time there was a shiny
spirit named Karly. She lived among the stars
with all sorts of other shiny spirits."

"One day," Natasha continued, "Karly-the-Spirit decided to come to Earth and be born as a human being. So she picked the perfect parents, and after nine months she was born inside a little, tiny baby."

"Hey," Karly giggled. "This story is about me, isn't it?"

"Yep," Natasha said.

"You see, when a spirit decides to live in a body, it forgets who it really is. So to help Karly remember, her special friend, Natasha — that's me — came to Earth to remind her."

Karly clapped her hands. "And now we play and laugh and eat lots of blueberry pie and chocolate swirl cookies."

Natasha nodded. "Always remember who you are... a beautiful, shiny spirit made of love and light."

Karly's smile grew bigger and bigger. "I can feel my spirit shining inside me!" she said, putting her hand over her heart.

"Your spirit helps you love yourself and everyone around you," Natasha said. "But it's easy to be distracted by the outside world and forget who you really are."

"You don't have to worry about me," Karly declared.
"I promise to remember."

"That's great!" Natasha said. "Then I guess it's time for me to go."

They hugged and Karly's eyes filled with tears. "Will I ever see you again?" she asked.

"Don't be sad," Natasha said. "I'll come back if you ever need me."

Karly waved goodbye as Natasha flew off to her home in the stars.

At first, Karly really missed Natasha, but as time went by it became harder and harder to remember her invisible friend.

She spent lots of time reading books and making up stories about dinosaurs, space ships and enchanted fairies. The kids at school teased her for being so quiet, and it was hard for Karly to make friends. Every day her heart felt heavier and heavier until all the magic that had once filled her life was gone.

One afternoon at the bus stop, two girls were picking on Karly. One grabbed her books and started a game of keep-away.

"Hey Karly-Barley!" she yelled. "Want to know why you don't have any friends?"

"Because you think you're smarter than everyone else," the other girl taunted.

Karly tried not to cry, but the tears slipped out anyway. She ran straight home to her bedroom and covered her face with her hands. "Why doesn't anyone like me?" she sobbed.

Suddenly there was a whoosh near Karly's window and she felt something bouncing beside her like a kangaroo. She looked up. "Who are you?" Karly asked.

"Don't you remember me? I'll give you a hint." The shiny being flopped onto the floor and rolled around and around like a leaf blowing in the wind.

"Natasha!" Karly yelled. Jumping up, she hugged her invisible friend and they danced around the room, fluttering like butterflies.

Then Karly stopped dancing and sat on the bed. "I'm not a very good friend," she said. "When I forgot about you, I forgot all about my spirit too. How will I ever get it back?"

Natasha held up a mirror and Karly saw that she was glowing brighter and brighter. "Hey!" she said. "It's still there!"

Suddenly, Karly felt her spirit warm inside her. "I never want to forget again!" she declared.

Natasha raised her eyebrows. "How will you remember?"

"Hmmm." Karly looked out the window and thought for a moment. Then she snapped her fingers. "I've got it!"

"I'll just live inside out," Karly said.

"What do you mean?"

"Since my spirit lives inside my heart, I want it to always shine through to the outside."

"Yes! Inside out!" Natasha sang. "That's a perfect way to let everyone know the real you."

Then Karly reached down and took off her shoes and socks.

"What are you doing?" Natasha asked.

Karly turned her socks inside out and put them on again. "From now on," she said, "I'm going to wear my socks like this so I'll always remember to live inside out."

"That's a great idea," Natasha said. "If I had feet, I'd wear my socks that way too."

For the rest of the day, Karly and Natasha laughed and played. They pretended to jump on clouds and walk on the moon. They bounced on the bed like kangaroos and rolled around like leaves blowing in the wind.

Karly's life was magical once again... and this time she was going to keep it that way.

ILLUMINATION
Arts

PUBLISHING COMPANY, INC.

P.O. Box 1865, Bellevue, WA 98009
Tel: 425-644-7185 ✳ 888-210-8216 (orders only) ✳ Fax: 425-644-9274
liteinfo@illumin.com ✳ www.illumin.com

Library of Congress Cataloging-in-Publication Data

Halley, Wendy Stofan, 1965-
    Inside Out / story by Wendy Stofan Halley ; illustrations by Roberta Collier-Morales.
      p. cm.
    Summary: With the help of her invisible friend, Karly is able to let her true self, her
shining spirit, shine through.
    ISBN 0-9701907-5-1
    [1. Spirit—Fiction.] I. Collier-Morales, Roberta, ill. II. Title.

PZ7.H15445 In 2003
[E]—dc21

                2002027513

Published in the United States of America
Printed in Singapore by Tien Wah Press
Book Designer: Molly Murrah, Murrah & Company, Kirkland, WA

ILLUMINATION ARTS PUBLISHING COMPANY, INC.
is a member of Publishers in Partnership – replanting our nation's forests.

The Illumination Arts Collection Of Inspiring Children's Books

ALL I SEE IS PART OF ME   by Chara M. Curtis, illustrated by Cynthia Aldrich
In this international bestseller, a child finds the light within his heart and his common link with all of life.

THE BONSAI BEAR   by Bernard Libster, illustrated by Aries Cheung
Issa uses bonsai methods to keep his pet bear small, but the playful cub dreams of following its true nature.

CASSANDRA'S ANGEL   by Gina Otto, illustrated by Trudy Joost
Cassandra feels lonely and misunderstood until a special angel guides her to the truth within.

CORNELIUS AND THE DOG STAR   by Diana Spyropulos, illustrated by Ray Williams
Grouchy old Cornelius Basset-Hound can't enter Dog Heaven until he learns about love, fun and kindness.

THE DOLL LADY   by H. Elizabeth Collins-Varni, illustrated by Judy Kuusisto
The doll lady teaches children to treat dolls kindly and with great love, for they are just like people.

DRAGON   written and illustrated by Jody Bergsma
Born on the same day, a gentle prince and a ferocious, fire-breathing dragon share a prophetic destiny.

DREAMBIRDS   by David Ogden, illustrated by Jody Bergsma
A Native American boy battles his own ego as he searches for the elusive dreambird and its powerful gift.

DREAMS TO GROW ON   by Christine Hurley Deriso, illustrated by Matthew Archambault
A young girl spends an entire day exploring the unlimited possibilities for her future.

FUN IS A FEELING   by Chara M. Curtis, illustrated by Cynthia Aldrich
Find your fun! "Fun isn't something or somewhere or who. It's a feeling of joy that lives inside of you."

HOW FAR TO HEAVEN?   by Chara M. Curtis, illustrated by Alfred Currier
Exploring the wonders of nature, Nanna and her granddaughter discover that heaven is all around them.

IN EVERY MOON THERE IS A FACE   by Charles Mathes, illustrated by Arlene Graston
The face of the moon invites a child on a wondrous journey of the imagination.

LITTLE SQUAREHEAD   by Peggy O'Neill, illustrated by Denise Freeman
Rosa overcomes the stigma of her unusual appearance after finding the glowing diamond within her heart.

THE LITTLE WIZARD   written and illustrated by Jody Bergsma
Young Kevin discovers a wizard's cloak while on a perilous mission to save his mother's life.

ONE SMILE   by Cindy McKinley, illustrated by Mary Gregg Byrne
Little Katie's innocent smile ignites a far-reaching circle of warmth and selfless giving.

THE RIGHT TOUCH   by Sandy Kleven, LCSW, illustrated by Jody Bergsma
This award-winning, read-aloud story teaches children how to prevent sexual abuse.

SKY CASTLE   by Sandra Hanken, illustrated by Jody Bergsma
Alive with dolphins, parrots and fairies, this magical tale inspires us to believe in the power of our dreams.

TO SLEEP WITH THE ANGELS   by H. Elizabeth Collins, illustrated by Judy Kuusisto
Comforting her to sleep each night, a young girl's guardian angel fills her dreams with magical adventures.

THE TREE   by Dana Lyons, illustrated by David Danioth
This powerful song of an ancient Douglas fir celebrates the age-old cycle of life in the Pacific Rain Forest.

WHAT IF…   by Regina J. Williams, illustrated by Doug Keith
Using his fantastic imagination, a little boy delays bedtime for as long as possible. Glow-in-the-dark page included.

THE WHOOSH OF GADOOSH   by Pat Skene, illustrated by Doug Keith
Gadoosh, a whimsical character without a home, inspires children to find the magic within their hearts.

WINGS OF CHANGE   by Franklin Hill, Ph.D., illustrated by Aries Cheung
A contented little caterpillar resists his approaching transformation into a butterfly.

www.illumin.com